WALLACE AND GRACE

and the Cupcake Caper

READ & BLOOM BOOKS

WALLACE AND GRACE

and the Cupcake Caper

Heather Alexander
illustrated by Laura Zarrin

BLOOMSBURY
CHILDREN'S BOOKS
NEW YORK LONDON OXFORD NEW DELHI SYDNEY

To ORS, whose messy nest may indeed
be a work of art! —H. A.

For my parents, Bill and Sharon Nienhaus, for
encouraging me to follow my dreams. —L. Z.

BLOOMSBURY CHILDREN'S BOOKS
Bloomsbury Publishing Inc., part of Bloomsbury Publishing Plc
1385 Broadway, New York, NY 10018

BLOOMSBURY, BLOOMSBURY CHILDREN'S BOOKS, and the Diana logo are trademarks of
Bloomsbury Publishing Plc

First published in the United States of America in May 2017 by Bloomsbury Children's Books
Paperback edition published in November 2018

Bloomsbury books may be purchased for business or promotional use. For information on bulk
purchases please contact Macmillan Corporate and Premium Sales Department at
specialmarkets@macmillan.com

ISBN 978-1-68119-011-2 (paperback)

The Library of Congress has cataloged the hardcover edition as follows:
Names: Alexander, Heather, author. | Zarrin, Laura, illustrator.
Title: Wallace and Grace and the cupcake caper / by Heather Alexander ; illustrated by Laura Zarrin.
Description: New York : Bloomsbury, 2017.
Summary: When Monty the chipmunk's cupcake is stolen, owl detectives
Wallace and Grace try to find "whoo-done-it."
Identifiers: LCCN 2016036833 (print) | LCCN 2016040985 (e-book)
ISBN 978-1-68119-010-5 (hardcover)
ISBN 978-1-68119-471-4 (e-book) • ISBN 978-1-68119-472-1 (e-PDF)
Subjects: | CYAC: Mystery and detective stories. | Owls—Fiction. | Forest animals—Fiction. |
BISAC: JUVENILE FICTION / Readers / Chapter Books. | JUVENILE FICTION /
Mysteries & Detective Stories. | JUVENILE FICTION / Animals / Birds.
Classification: LCC PZ7.A37717 Wag 2017 (print) | LCC PZ7.A37717 (e-book) | DDC [Fic]—dc23
LC record available at https://lccn.loc.gov/2016036833

Art created with Blackwing pencils and Photoshop
Typeset in Burbank, Century Schoolbook, and Roger • Book design by John Candell
Printed in China by C&C Offset Printing Co., Ltd., Shenzhen, Guangdong
3 5 7 9 10 8 6 4

To find out more about our authors and books visit www.bloomsbury.com and sign up for our newsletters.

Table of Contents

CHAPTER 1
Eye Spy

"Let's play a game," said Wallace.
He flew high above the trees.

"Let's play I Spy," said Grace.
She flew next to him.

"I spy with my little eye
something blue," called Wallace.

"What's blue?" Grace looked

down. "Everything is green and brown."

Spring was starting in the Great Woods. Green leaves bloomed on brown tree trunks.

"Look and see!" Wallace did a loop-the-loop in the sky.

"That's it! The sky is blue," said Grace.

"The sky isn't blue *yet*. Just saying." Wallace liked to point these things out.

Grace sighed. Wallace was right. The sky was still dark. It was *very* early morning. The sky would turn blue later, when they were asleep.

Wallace and Grace slept in the day. They worked at night. Owls do that.

"Here's a hint," said Wallace.
"Down, not up."

Grace looked down.

She spotted a pink earthworm
poking up from the dirt.

She spotted a bird

with red

wings

in a

nest.

"Do you give up?" asked Wallace.

Grace *hated* to give up. But she didn't see anything blue.

Wallace swooped low. Grace followed.

And there was a teeny tiny blue flower. Wallace was very tricky!

"Ta-da!" cried Wallace.

Grace picked the flower and gave it a long sniff.

Wallace slurped up the pink earthworm.

"Thief! Thief!" someone called.

"Listen up!" cried Wallace.

Grace put her wing to her ear. The sound was far off. But owl ears are super good.

"Thief! Thief!" They heard it again.

"Someone needs our help," said Grace.

"Eeeyoy!" cried Wallace. "Let's go!"

Wallace and Grace were best friends. They were also detectives. They solved mysteries. They

ran the Night Owl Detective
Agency. They always found out
whooo-done-it.

Wallace and Grace circled the
sky over the Great Woods. Who
was calling?

"Down below!"
called Grace.
They flew
to an empty
picnic table.

"Took you
detectives

long enough," grumbled Monty the chipmunk. He stood on a nearby log. His little arms were crossed.

"Do you need our help?" asked Wallace.

"I most certainly do," said Monty. "Someone took my cupcake."

"Your cupcake?" Grace could go for a cupcake. She liked frosting more than earthworms. "Are you sure?"

"Most certainly. It was right here." Monty pointed inside the hollow log. "Now it is not here. And I know who stole it."

"You do?" Wallace sighed. He had been hoping for a mystery. Now there was no mystery.

"Sal stole it. Sal is a thief!" cried Monty.

"Say what?" Sal popped out of his hole. His groundhog fur stuck up. He had a serious case of bed head. "I did not steal anything."

"Yes, you did." Little Monty
stood nose-to-nose with Sal.

Monty was fierce—even for a
chipmunk.

"Whoa, everyone calm down."
Wallace stepped between them.

"Monty, why do you think it was
Sal?" asked Grace.

Grace was good at asking
questions.

"Right before our winter nap,
a boy had a birthday party here."
Monty pointed to the picnic table.
"There was singing. And presents.
And food. I love parties!"

"What about the cupcake?"
Wallace liked to get the facts.

"A cupcake was left over. So I
took it," said Monty.

"And I asked for a taste," said Sal. "But Monty said no. He put the cupcake inside the log."

"I was saving it for my wake-up treat," explained Monty.

"Then what happened?" asked Wallace.

"We both went to sleep," said Sal.

"When I woke up, my cupcake was gone." Monty looked at Sal.

"Hey, don't look at me. I was asleep, too!" cried Sal.

"They were hibernating," Grace told Wallace. "*Hibernating* is a big word for sleeping all winter." Grace loved using big words.

"I know all about hibernating. I also know groundhogs wake up on February second to look for their shadow." Wallace poked Sal.

"*You* were awake while Monty was asleep."

"I did wake up. I saw my shadow. I went back to sleep," said Sal. "Beginning, middle, and end of story."

"Thief!" cried Monty again.

"Please take my case, Wallace and Grace." Sal folded his groundhog paws together. "I need you to prove that I did *not* steal Monty's cupcake."

"These detectives are mine, Sal." Monty puffed out his chipmunk cheeks. "And I need them to prove that you certainly *did* steal my cupcake."

"Two new cases!" said Wallace.

"Whose case will we take?" asked Grace.

17

They needed a private Partner
Talk.

"I think Sal did it," said Grace.
"He wanted the cupcake. He had
the perfect time to take it, while
Monty was asleep."

"I don't think Sal did it. There's no evidence, or proof, that it was him," Wallace pointed out.

"We need to investigate," said Grace.

"We need more facts," said Wallace.

"Wallace and Grace will take *both* cases!" said Grace.

CHAPTER 2
Eyewitness

First, Wallace and Grace needed to know what the cupcake looked like to find it. "Describe the cupcake," Wallace told Monty.

"It was the prettiest—" began Monty.

"Hold up." Wallace stopped him.

"Give the facts and only the facts."

"Yellow cake. Pink frosting," said Monty.

"Here's a clue!" Grace found a smear of pink frosting in the hollow log.

Wallace opened his little detective notebook. He  wrote all clues there:

Clue #1: Frosting in log.

Grace looked for more frosting. She turned her head all the way around. Owls can do that.

"Aha!" she cried.

A blob of pink frosting. Right by the hole where Sal lived!

Grace pulled out her little magnifying glass. She peered through it. It made everything look much bigger.

"I see a paw print in this frosting," she said. "A *groundhog* print."

Sal gulped. He hid his hands behind his back.

This was not looking good for Sal.

Wallace wrote: **Clue #2: Frosting print at Sal's home.**

"That's evidence that Sal did it," said Grace.

"I knew it!" cried Monty.

"Okay, okay," said Sal. "I *did* swipe my paw in the frosting. But then I saw my shadow."

"That means six more weeks of winter," said Grace. She knew things like this.

"I hate winter. I went right back to sleep. I left the cupcake in the log." Sal raised his little finger. "Pinkie promise."

Monty refused to link pinkies. "I do not believe you."

"Groundhog's honor," said Sal. "I did not eat the cupcake."

"*Hmmm*," said Wallace. Wallace always said "*Hmmm*" when he was thinking. "We need to find a witness."

"What's a witness?" asked Monty.

"Someone who saw Sal that day. A witness can prove he is telling the truth," said Wallace.

"Me, me, me!" Nisha the snake slithered out from under the log. "I was here on Groundhog's Day."

Witness #1: Nisha, wrote Wallace in his notebook.

Everyone gathered around. Nisha smiled. She liked attention.

"I heard Sal wake up. Then I heard him lick his lips by the log." She pointed at Sal. "He did it!"

Sal gulped. Things were *really* not looking good.

"Hold up," said Wallace. "You *heard* Sal. But what did you *see*?"

"Nothing. My eyes were closed. Snakes hibernate, too. We need beauty rest." Nisha tilted her head. "Why?"

"You never *saw* Sal. Maybe you heard someone else," said Wallace.

"Or if it was Sal, maybe he didn't eat the cupcake. Maybe he licked his lips to taste the frosting," said Grace. "Or maybe he was licking up drool."

"I do not drool!" cried Sal.

"We need an *eye*witness. That's a witness who *saw* what Sal did," said Wallace.

"What about Scarlet?" Grace looked up. "She is always in her tree. Cardinals do not hibernate."

Witness #2: Scarlet, wrote Wallace.

Wallace and Grace flew up, up, up. They landed on a branch above Scarlet's nest. The branch creaked.

31

"Shhh!" warned Scarlet. She covered her two eggs. "My babies will hatch soon. Go away!"

What a messy nest, thought Wallace.

Many things were woven into the twigs. He quickly wrote a list in his notebook.

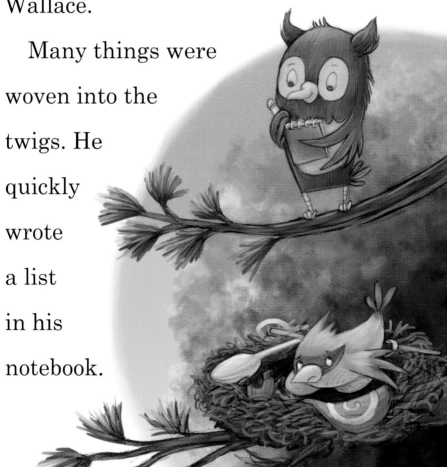

Plastic spoon

Swirled paper

Chopstick

Long shoelace

Half an action figure

"Where were you on the morning of February second?" Grace asked Scarlet.

"Right here," said Scarlet. "Now shoo! I need to sit on my eggs."

Grace didn't shoo. "Did you see Sal? Did you see him eat a cupcake?"

"I saw Sal. But the groundhog only swiped the frosting," said Scarlet. "He did not eat the cupcake."

Suddenly, there was a loud c-c-c-rack!

"Wings in the air, Grace!" cried Wallace.

They flew off just in time. The branch snapped in half!

"Detective work can be dangerous," said Grace.

"Do you want to quit?" asked
Wallace. He hoped not. They were
good partners.

"Never!" said Grace.

They went back to Monty and Sal. Nisha had slithered away.

"Scarlet was a good eyewitness," Wallace reported. "Sal is telling the truth."

"Whooot-whooot!" sang Grace. "We solved both cases!"

Shake, shake, flap, flap.

Grace did her celebration dance. Sal joined in. Sal was a smooth dancer.

Monty let out a whistle. "Stop the party!"

Grace stopped dancing. So did Sal.

"I want answers. Who stole my cupcake, if it wasn't Sal?" asked Monty.

"You are right. We still have detective work to do," said Wallace.

No case was over until Wallace and Grace knew *all* the answers.

They looked inside the log again.

"Eeeyoy!" Wallace spotted a line of black ants marching out of the log.

And they were eating crumbs.

Yellow cupcake crumbs!

"Follow those ants!" said Grace.

CHAPTER 3
Master of Tricky

Grace went first. Then Wallace.
Then Monty. Then Sal.

They followed the parade of ants.

It was hard not to step on them.
Or eat them.

"Someone ate my cupcake," said
Monty. "And left only crumbs."

Clue #3: Crumbs, wrote Wallace.

"The ants will bring us to the thief," said Wallace.

The ants led them into a field of flowers.

And then . . . nothing.

No cupcake. No thief.

They had reached a dead end.

The sun rose. The sky turned blue. It was time for owls to go to sleep.

But Wallace *really* wanted to solve the case before bedtime.

He had to hurry.

Then they saw it.

A fluffy red tail poked out of the flowers.

"We found the culprit," whispered Grace.

"What culprit? I found a red fox," said Wallace.

"*Culprit* is a big word for cupcake thief," said Grace.

"You could have just said that." Wallace turned to Monty. "That red fox stole your cupcake."

"Most certainly," said Monty.

"Let's get him." Wallace was excited. They *would* solve this case before bedtime!

"How will we catch him? A red fox is tricky," said Grace.

45

"I have a plan," said Wallace. "I am the Master of Tricky."

He had Grace, Monty, and Sal make a circle around the fox.

One . . . two . . . three . . .

"Gotcha!" they all yelled.

The red fox cried out in surprise. Two owls, a chipmunk, and a groundhog jumped on top of him!

"We caught the thief!" called Wallace.

"Get off! Get off!" cried the fox. Then he karate-kicked Sal.

"Ow!" Sal backed away.

"You stole my cupcake." Monty
wasn't afraid of Karate Fox.

But the fox hadn't taken the
cupcake. He wasn't the thief.

Wallace and Grace had made a mistake.

Grace groaned. "We jumped to a conclusion."

"No, I think we jumped on a fox," said Sal.

"Jumping to a conclusion is deciding whooo-done-it *without* all the facts," explained Grace.

"We had no evidence," agreed Wallace.

They had been in too big a rush to solve the case.

They needed to slow down.

Grace put on her sunglasses. So did Wallace. They would solve the case in the sunshine. They would stay awake until they found the cupcake thief.

"Let's do this the right way."

Wallace turned to a new page in his notebook. "Let's find clues."

"Have you seen a cupcake?" Grace asked the fox.

"No," said the fox. "I am looking for my missing things."

"You have missing things, too?" asked Wallace. This was interesting. "Like what?"

The fox held up a high-top sneaker. "The shoelace is gone."

The fox also had a chopstick. "I used to have two."

The fox held up the top half of an action figure. "This guy is missing his legs."

Wallace wrote everything in his notebook.

Grace reached for his notebook. She flipped back a page.

Plastic spoon

Swirled paper

Chopstick

Long shoelace

Half an action figure

"Aha!" she cried.

"Aha what?" asked Wallace.

"Let's play I Spy," said Grace.

"Now?" Monty threw up his arms. "I hired you owls to solve my case. Not to play games."

"This game will lead to the thief," promised Grace.

CHAPTER 4
Look and See

"I spy something with purple-and-white swirls," said Grace.

"Where?" Wallace didn't see purple-and-white swirls in the Great Woods.

"Here's a hint," said Grace. "Up, not down."

Wallace looked up. He still didn't see anything.

"Give up?" asked Grace.

"Never," said Wallace.

"Wait!" Monty bounced on his chipmunk toes. "The cupcake's wrapper had purple-and-white swirls!"

"You never told us that, Monty," Wallace said. "You didn't give *all* the facts."

"Oops. My bad." Monty didn't think the color of the cupcake wrapper was an important fact.

But it was.

And now Wallace knew what Grace knew.

"Eeeyoy!" he cried. "Find the purple-and-white swirls, find the thief. Wings in the air!"

The two owls flew high in the sky.

"Hey! We don't have wings!" called Monty.

Wallace and Grace landed by Scarlet's nest.

"Don't bother my babies," said Scarlet. Her two eggs had just hatched.

"You can't keep shooing us away," said Wallace. "We know you are the thief."

"You saw Sal swipe the frosting," said Grace. "But then he went back to sleep. And *you* took the cupcake."

"You have no proof," said Scarlet.

"Yes, we do." Wallace pointed to the purple-and-white-swirl cupcake wrapper. It was woven into the nest. He had seen it earlier.

Clue #4: Cupcake wrapper in nest, wrote Wallace in his notebook.

Scarlet's face turned red. "I wanted the pretty wrapper. So I ate the cupcake."

"Why?" asked Wallace.

"Look and see," cried Grace. "She's an artist."

Wallace took a closer look at

Scarlet's nest.

Before, he saw messy.

Now, he saw amazing!

A work of modern art.

"Wow!" said Wallace. Then he
tugged the shoelace with his beak.
"But you stole this from the fox.
You stole a lot of things."

"It was all in the name of art."
Scarlet hung her head. "I'm sorry."

"You can't steal," said Wallace.
"You need to give everything back."

"Poor Monty," said Grace. "She
can't give back his cupcake."

Right then, the baby birds began
to sing. Wallace had an idea.

"She can give Monty something
else," he said.

A little later, they flew Monty
and Sal to the nest.

Flying was tricky—with a

chipmunk and groundhog on their backs!

"Look! No hands!" cried Sal.

On the way, Grace told Monty that Scarlet was the thief. But she didn't tell him about the surprise.

"It's a birthday party for the baby birds," cried Grace.

"There's singing!" cried Monty.

"And dancing," said Sal.

"And presents," said Scarlet.

Grace handed Monty the purple-and-white-swirl cupcake wrapper. It was filled with nuts and berries.

"Yum!" cried Monty. "I love parties even more than cupcakes."

"Case solved," said Wallace. He gave Grace a high five.

"Two cases solved," said Grace.

"Time for bed." Wallace yawned.

"Not yet," said Grace. "I want another turn. I spy something red."

"Scarlet's wing!" This game was way too easy for Wallace.

"No." Grace grinned.

"*Hmmm.*" Wallace looked and looked and looked. "I can't find it."

Grace had tricked the Master of Tricky!

"I need a clue," said Wallace.

"The *back* of the clue is in *front* of you." Grace could be tricky, too.

Wallace looked closer. Then he clapped his wings together. "Now I see him!"

"Good detectives follow the clues," said Grace.

"Always," agreed Wallace.

Wallace and Grace were very good detectives.

READ & BLOOM

Agnes and Clarabelle are the best of friends!

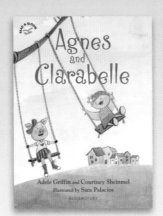

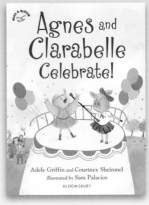

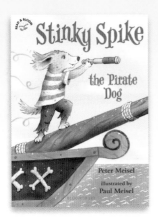

Stinky Spike can sniff his way out of any trouble!

You don't want to miss these great characters! The Read & Bloom line is perfect for newly independent readers. These stories are fully illustrated and bursting with fun!

Caveboy is always ready for an adventure!

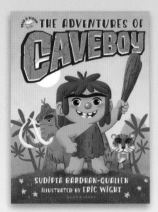

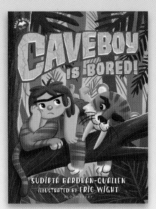

Wallace and Grace are owl detectives who solve mysteries!

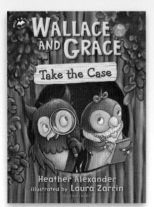

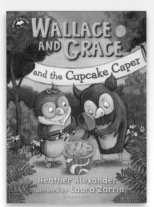

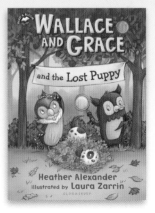

 www.bloomsbury.com • Twitter: BloomsburyKids • Facebook: KidsBloomsbury

Heather Alexander is the author of many books for young readers. She grew up by the woods in New Jersey and found deer, fox, turkeys, rabbits, and the occasional owl detective in her yard. She now lives in Los Angeles.

www.heatheralexanderbooks.com

Laura Zarrin is an illustrator by day and a detective by night. She is often called upon to solve mysteries for her family. She's been known to find lost shoes and lost homework and to discover who ate the last chocolate chip cookie. When she's not solving mysteries, she spends her time drawing, reading, drinking really strong iced tea, and eating fig Newtons. She lives in Northern California with her husband, their two sons, and her assistant, Cody the Chihuahua.

www.laurazarrinstudios.com